Here's what kids have to say about reading Magic Tree House® books and Magic Tree House® Merlin Missions:

Thank you for writing these great books! I have learned a great deal of information about history and the world around me.—Rosanna

Your series, the Magic Tree House, was really influential on my late childhood years. [Jack and Annie] taught me courage through their rigorous adventures and profound friendship, and how they stuck it out through thick and thin, from start to finish.—Joe

Your description is fantastic! The words pop out... oh, man... [the Magic Tree House series] is really exciting!—Christina

I like the Magic Tree House series. I stay up all night reading them. Even on school nights!—Peter

I think I've read about twenty-five of your Magic Tree House books! I'm reading every Magic Tree House book I can get my hands on!—Jack

Never stop writing, and if you can't think about anything to write about, don't worry, use some of my ideas!!—Kevin

Parents, teachers, and librarians love Magic Tree House® books, too!

[Magic Tree House] comes up quite a bit at parent/teacher conferences. . . . The parents are amazed at how much more reading is being done at home because of your books. I am very pleased to know such fun and interesting reading exists for students. . . . Your books have also made students want to learn more about the places Jack and Annie visit. What wonderful starters for some research projects!—Kris L.

As a librarian, I have seen many happy young readers coming into the library to check out the next Magic Tree House book in the series. I have assisted young library patrons with finding nonfiction materials related to the Magic Tree House book they have read. . . . The message you are sending to children is invaluable: siblings can be friends; boys and girls can hang out together. . . .—Lynne H.

[My daughter] had a slow start reading, but somehow with your Magic Tree House series, she has been inspired and motivated to read. It is with such urgency that she tracks down your books. She often blurts out various facts and lines followed by "I read that in my Magic Tree House book."—Jenny E.

[My students] seize every opportunity they can to reread a Magic Tree House book or look at all the wonderful illustrations. Jack and Annie have opened a door to a world of literacy that I know will continue throughout the lives of my students.—Deborah H.

[My son] carries his Magic Tree House books everywhere he goes. He just can't put the book he is reading down until he finishes it. . . . He is doing better in school overall since he has made reading a daily thing. He even has a bet going with his aunt that if he continues doing well in school, she will continue to buy him the next book in the Magic Tree House series.—Rosalie R.

MAGIC TREE HOUSE® #37
A MERLIN MISSION

Dragon
of the
Red Dawn

by Mary Pope Osborne

illustrated by Sal Murdocca

A STEPPING STONE BOOK™

Random House 🏠 New York

Grateful acknowledgment is made to Doubleday, a division of Random House, Inc., for permission to reprint the translation of Basho's haiku found on page 282 of *From the Country of Eight Islands* by Hiroaki Sato and Burton Watson, copyright © 1981 by Hiroaki Sato and Burton Watson. Used by permission of Doubleday, a division of Random House, Inc.

Published in the United States by Random House Children's Books, a division of Random House, Inc., 1745 Broadway, New York, NY 10019. Originally published in hardcover by Random House Children's Books, a division of Random House, Inc., in 2007.

Random House and colophon are registered trademarks and A Stepping Stone Book and colophon are trademarks of Random House, Inc. Magic Tree House is a registered trademark of Mary Pope Osborne; used under license.

Visit us on the Web! www.randomhouse.com/kids
www.magictreehouse.com

Educators and librarians, for a variety of teaching tools, visit us at
www.randomhouse.com/teachers

The Library of Congress has cataloged the hardcover edition of this work as follows:
Osborne, Mary Pope.
Dragon of the red dawn / by Mary Pope Osborne ; illustrated by Sal Murdocca.
  p. cm. — (Magic tree house ; #37)
"A Merlin mission."
"A Stepping Stone book."
Summary: When Merlin is weighed down by sorrows, Jack and Annie travel back to feudal Japan to learn one of the four secrets of happiness.
ISBN 978-0-375-83727-2 (trade) — ISBN 978-0-375-93727-9 (lib. bdg.) —
ISBN 978-0-375-83728-9 (pbk.)
[1. Time travel—Fiction. 2. Magic—Fiction. 3. Happiness—Fiction.
4. Brothers and sisters—Fiction.
5. Japan—History—Tokugawa period, 1600–1868—Fiction.]
I. Murdocca, Sal, ill. II. Title.
PZ7.O81167Dr 2007 [Fic]—dc22 2006017188

Printed in the United States of America
22

For Griffin Loehr van Rhyn,
a good friend of Jack and Annie's

Dear Reader,

*F*or many years, I have admired Japan's literature and art. I collect books of Japanese poetry, and I also collect books of old Japanese prints that show people going about their everyday lives. Japanese art and poetry were my inspiration for writing this book, because I wanted to live in the scenes the artists and poets created. I wanted to ride on a fishing boat, sip tea in a teahouse, see cherry-blossom petals float down a river. When I'm writing a book, I feel as if I am living in another time and place. Working on this particular Magic Tree House adventure, I couldn't wait to get to my writing desk every day . . . to visit the world of my dreams.

Mary Pope Osborne

CONTENTS

Now I shall dream,
Lulled by the patter of rain
And the song of the frogs.
    —poem from old Japan,
translated by Lafcadio Hearn

Prologue

One summer day in Frog Creek, Pennsylvania, a mysterious tree house appeared in the woods. A brother and sister named Jack and Annie soon learned that the tree house was magic—it could take them to any time and any place in history. They also learned that the tree house belonged to Morgan le Fay, a magical librarian from the legendary realm of Camelot.

After Jack and Annie traveled on many adventures for Morgan, Merlin the magician began sending them on "Merlin Missions" in the tree house. With help from two young sorcerers named Teddy and Kathleen, Jack and Annie visited four *mythical* places and found valuable objects to help save Camelot.

On their next four Merlin Missions, Jack and Annie once again traveled to real times and real places in history: Venice, Baghdad, Paris, and New York City. After they proved to Merlin that they knew how to use magic wisely, he awarded them the Wand of Dianthus, a powerful magic wand that will help them make their own magic.

Jack and Annie are now waiting to hear from Merlin again. . . .

CHAPTER ONE

For Merlin's Sake

Tap, tap, tap.

Jack was dreaming that a white bird was pecking at his window. *Tap . . . tap.* A red bird appeared and pecked with the white bird. *Tap . . . tap.*

"Jack, wake up!" said Annie.

Jack opened his eyes.

"They're here!" said Annie.

"Who? The birds?" said Jack.

"No! Teddy and Kathleen!" Annie rushed to the window and waved outside. "They're tossing pebbles at our windows."

"Teddy and Kathleen!" Jack jumped out of bed and joined Annie at the window.

The two young enchanters of Camelot were standing in Jack and Annie's front yard. They were dressed in long, dark cloaks. They smiled and waved up at Jack and Annie.

"Merlin must have sent them!" said Jack.

Teddy made a walking motion with his fingers and pointed toward the Frog Creek woods.

Annie nodded eagerly. "They want us to meet them at the tree house!" she said to Jack. "Hurry and get dressed! Before Mom and Dad wake up!"

Annie started out of Jack's room. When she got to the door, she turned. "Oh, and don't forget to bring the Wand of Dianthus!"

Jack threw on his clothes. He grabbed his backpack and peeked inside. The wand was there. Jack put his pack on his back. Then he slipped quietly downstairs and out the door.

Annie was standing on the front porch. "Let's go!" she said.

Jack and Annie ran across their yard and dashed up the sidewalk.

"I wonder why they came for us!" said Annie.

"I wonder where we're going!" said Jack.

"I wonder *everything*!" said Annie.

Jack and Annie crossed the street and hurried into the Frog Creek woods. The early-March trees looked weary from winter, gray and brown with no leaves on them yet.

"Look—" said Annie, out of breath. "They're waiting for us!"

Jack looked up. Teddy and Kathleen were waving from the window of the magic tree house.

Jack grabbed the rope ladder and started up. Annie followed. When Jack and Annie climbed inside the tree house, they threw their arms around Teddy and Kathleen.

"We're so glad to see you!" cried Annie.

"And we are happy to see you, also," said Kathleen. The sea girl's lovely water-blue eyes sparkled.

"Indeed," said Teddy. "It has been too long."

"What's our mission this time?" asked Jack. "Where's Merlin sending us?"

Teddy glanced at Kathleen. "I fear Merlin does not even know we are here," said Teddy. "We have come not at his bidding, but for his sake."

"What does *that* mean?" asked Jack.

"Merlin is not well," said Kathleen. "He complains that he is getting old and feeble and that life is full of sorrows. He does not eat or sleep."

"Oh, no!" said Annie.

"All of Camelot wishes to help him," said Teddy. "But no one knows quite how."

"What can *we* do to help?" asked Jack.

Teddy picked up a book from the corner of the tree house. "Throughout the ages, people all over the world have sought the secrets of happiness," he said. "Morgan wants you to search for four of these secrets to share with Merlin. She believes that the first one might be found *here*."

Jack took the book from Teddy. He read the title aloud.

"Oh, wow, we've been to Japan before!" said Annie.

"Before we met you," Jack said to Teddy and Kathleen. "We had an adventure with ninjas."

"Yes, Morgan told us," said Teddy. "But she said that on that journey, you visited the country-side. This time you must travel to the capital city."

"Are you guys coming with us?" asked Annie.

"I am afraid not," said Kathleen. "We must return to Camelot now to help Morgan. Since

Merlin has fallen ill, she has taken on much of his work."

"You have the wand, do you not?" asked Teddy.

"Yep," said Jack. He reached into his backpack and took out the Wand of Dianthus. The spiraled wand was shaped like a unicorn's horn.

"*With the help of the wand, you will make your own magic*," said Teddy.

"That's what Merlin said when he gave it to us," said Annie.

"But he didn't say *how*," said Jack.

"It is very simple," said Teddy. "The wand has three rules. First, it only works for the good of others. The wand can never be used for selfish reasons."

"Second, the wand works only after you have tried your very hardest without its help," said Kathleen. "Do not attempt to use its magic too quickly."

"And third, the wand only works with a command of five words," said Teddy. "So you must choose your words carefully."

"Can we review all that, please?" asked Jack.

"Don't worry, I've got it," said Annie. "We have to go. We have to help Merlin as soon as we can."

"If the tree house takes us to Japan, how will you go back to Camelot?" Jack asked Teddy and Kathleen.

Teddy and Kathleen held up their hands. They each wore a sparkling blue ring. "Our magic rings will take us home," said Kathleen.

"And this book from Camelot's library will bring *you* back home to Frog Creek," said Teddy, "after you have completed your mission." He picked up another book lying in a corner. It was the book about Pennsylvania that Jack and Annie had used on their first magic tree house adventures.

"Thanks," said Jack.

"Good-bye," said Annie. "Take good care of Merlin."

"We will try," said Kathleen. She and Teddy raised their magic rings to their lips. They whispered words too softly for Jack and Annie to hear, then blew on the rings. As they blew, the young sorcerers began to fade into the cool morning air. In a moment, they had disappeared completely.

Silence filled the tree house.

Annie turned to Jack. "Ready?" she said.

Jack nodded. He pointed to the cover of the Japan book. "I wish we could go *there*!" he said.

The tree house started to spin.

It spun faster and faster.

Then everything was still.

Absolutely still.

CHAPTER TWO

The Imperial Garden

Jack opened his eyes. Soft morning light shone across the floor of the tree house. Pink flowers bloomed on a branch outside the window.

Jack and Annie were wearing brown baggy pants and brown silk robes with blue sashes. On their feet were stiff white socks and straw sandals. Jack's backpack had turned into a burlap bag.

"Are we wearing bathrobes?" asked Jack.

"I think they're called kimonos," said Annie.

"Oh, right," said Jack. "Where'd we land exactly?" Jack and Annie looked out the window.

Below the tree house was a beautiful garden filled with cherry trees and long-leafed willows. A waterfall tumbled into a sparkling green pool.

"Wow," said Annie.

Jack opened the Japan book and found a painting that looked like the garden. He read aloud to Annie:

> In the 1600s, the Imperial Garden surrounded the Imperial Palace in the capital city of Japan. The city was called Edo (say EE-doh). In the mid-1800s, its name was changed to Tokyo (say TOH-kee-oh).

"Tokyo?" said Annie. "I've always wanted to go to Tokyo!"

"Me too," said Jack. He read on:

> The late 1600s in Japan were years of peace and prosperity. Art and culture thrived. But it was a time when the country was completely closed to the outside world. No one was allowed to

come in. The citizens of Edo were frequently checked to make sure they had passports.

"What's a passport exactly?" said Annie.

"It's an official booklet that says who you are," said Jack. "It also lists the different countries you traveled to." He read more:

Anyone who did not have a passport was considered a spy and punished severely.

"Uh-oh," said Annie. "We don't have passports."

"Yeah, that's a problem," said Jack.

"Hey! What if we use the Wand of Dianthus to *make* passports?" said Annie.

"Good idea!" said Jack. He peeked inside his bag. Good, the Wand of Dianthus was there.

"Wait, wait," said Annie. "We can't. Remember the rules. We can only use the magic wand for the good of *others*."

"Oh, right," said Jack.

"And we have to try our hardest before we use the wand," said Annie.

"We haven't tried anything yet," said Jack.

"I guess we should just start looking for a secret of happiness and hope no one catches us," said Annie.

"Shh," said Jack, "listen."

A bell was ringing in the distance. The ringing grew louder. Then came the sound of horses. Jack and Annie crouched down. They raised their heads just high enough to peek out the window. Through the flowery tree branches, they saw a small procession coming through the garden.

The man leading the procession was ringing a bell. Two men walked behind him, holding up banners. Behind them, four men rode slowly on horseback. They all wore baggy trousers and puffy shirts. Their heads were shaved, except for knots of black hair. Each had two swords—a long one and a short one—hanging from his belt.

At the very end of the procession rode a man in a billowing purple robe and a small purple hat. Red tassels hung from the bridle of his large black horse.

Jack looked at their research book again. He found a picture that looked like the man on the black horse. He read the caption to himself:

In the 1600s, the military ruler known as the shogun (say SHOW-gun) lived in the center of the Imperial Garden in a palace that had hundreds of rooms.

"That last guy is a *shogun*," Jack whispered to Annie. "He lives in a big palace in the garden." He kept reading:

> **Often the shogun's warriors traveled with him. They were called samurai (say SAM-uh-rye).**

"Oh, man," whispered Jack. "Those other guys are samurai!" He and Annie had barely escaped an armored samurai on their earlier trip to Japan.

> **Samurai were excellent horsemen well trained in the arts of fighting. The code of the samurai was strict. Samurai did not show their feelings. They had great powers of concentration.**

"They're gone," said Annie.

Jack looked out the window. The shogun and his samurai warriors had disappeared down a tree-shaded dirt road.

"We should get out of the Imperial Garden

fast," said Jack. "If we stay here, we're just asking to be caught."

"How do we get out?" asked Annie.

Jack looked in the Japan book. He found a map of Edo. "Look," he said, pointing at the map. "We have to get over this bridge that leads away from the Imperial Garden into the city. The bridge is on the east side of the garden."

"The morning sun is over there," said Annie, squinting into the sunlight. "So that must be east. Let's climb down and head that way."

"Good plan. Then we'll be walking in the opposite direction of those samurai," said Jack.

"Right," said Annie. She started down the rope ladder.

"Be careful," said Jack. "We don't want anyone to see us sneaking around the Imperial Garden."

Jack put the Japan book into his burlap bag and slung the bag over his shoulder. As he stepped onto the ladder, he nearly tripped on his kimono. "Oh, brother," he said. He held up the cloth and carefully climbed down.

Jack joined Annie on a wide path. A gust of dry wind carried petals from cherry trees through the air. The long branches of the willows swayed over the grass.

Jack and Annie began heading east, keeping their eyes and ears open for more people. They walked past flower beds and big rocks. They walked around a pond with swans. They started down a narrow lane between blossoming cherry trees.

Just as they came out from under the trees, Jack and Annie saw four men strolling toward them. One man was shorter and older than the others. He wore a straw hat and a tattered brown coat and used a walking stick. The other three had shaved heads with topknots, and two swords hung from each of their belts.

"Samurai!" whispered Jack.

"Yikes," said Annie.

"Run!" said Jack.

Jack and Annie turned around and started running back down the narrow lane.

Jack heard the men running after them. "Halt!" cried a samurai.

Jack grabbed Annie's hand and they stumbled to a halt. Out of breath, they turned to face the three samurai who were rushing toward them.

"Who are you?" one of the samurai barked. He was holding up his sword. "Why do you run from us? Are you spies?"

Just as Jack was about to answer, he heard a voice shout, "Baku! Koto!"

The man with the walking stick and straw hat was hurrying toward them. "Baku, Koto, what are you doing here?" he called out to Jack and Annie. "Why did you not wait for me at the bridge?"

CHAPTER THREE

Basho

The three samurai turned to the man with the walking stick. "You know them, Master?" one asked.

"Yes, of course," the man said. "This boy and girl are Baku and Koto, my best students."

"Hi, Master!" said Annie, pretending she knew who the man was. "We couldn't find the bridge, so we—uh—we—"

"We came here to look for you," said Jack.

"And now you have found me," said the man. "I am sorry you were frightened by my friends."

The samurai put away his sword. "Forgive
me," he said, bowing before Jack and Annie.

"Sure, no problem," said Annie.

The samurai turned to the small man. "We will leave you with your students now," he said. "Thank you, Most Honored Master, for your visit with us today." All three warriors bowed deeply before the man. Then they walked away.

Why did the samurai call the small man "Most Honored Master"? Jack wondered.

When the samurai were gone, the man turned to Jack and Annie. His eyes twinkled. "I believe you are safe now," he said.

"Thanks," said Annie. "But I'm afraid we're not Baku and Koto."

"No, you are not," said the man. "But you are not spies, either, are you?"

"No," said Jack.

"I did not think so," said the man. "That is why I thought you needed my help."

"Thank you," said Jack.

"You are most welcome," said the man. "Now perhaps you will tell me who you really are, and how you came to be here in the Imperial Garden."

"Our names are Jack and Annie," said Jack. "And we—" He paused. It seemed impossible to explain: Teddy and Kathleen's visit, Merlin's sorrow, Morgan's research book.

"We came here to search for a secret of happiness," said Annie.

The man smiled. "I believe that is something we all seek," he said. "But you must be very careful, Jack and Annie. The shogun does not allow foreigners into our country. If you do not have passports, you could be caught and punished."

"We know," said Annie. "What should we do?"

"Perhaps you should travel with me today," said the man. "You can continue to be my students, Baku and Koto."

"Good plan!" said Jack.

"You must remember, seek harmony with your surroundings," said the man. "Observe the people of Edo and do as they do. If you do not stand out, you will not be noticed by the samurai."

"Got it," said Annie.

Seek harmony with your surroundings. Observe the people of Edo and do as they do, Jack repeated to himself.

"Come," said the man. He started walking briskly through the garden.

Jack and Annie hurried after him. "Excuse me, but what's your name?" Annie said.

"My friends call me Basho," the man answered.

"Basho? That's a cute name!" said Annie.

"And why did the samurai call you 'Most Honored Master'?" asked Jack.

"Because I am their teacher," said Basho.

"What do you teach them?" asked Jack.

Basho smiled. "Today they learned how to listen to a cricket in a woodpile," he said, "and how to think like a frog."

"Cool," said Jack. *Those must be warrior skills*, he thought, *special ways to listen for an enemy or jump around with a sword*. He remembered how ninjas used secrets of nature to fight their enemies.

Basho led Jack and Annie through a wooden gate in a high wall. They walked over a wide stone bridge that crossed a moat. When they came to the other side of the bridge, they followed a path that led to a small boat dock on a river.

Three fishermen were loading wicker baskets into a long flat-bottomed boat. Hundreds of shiny little fish were inside each basket.

Basho walked over to the fishermen. "Good morning," he said.

"Good morning, Master Basho," the fishermen said. All of them bowed.

Everyone seems to know Basho, Jack thought.

"May my students and I ride with you down the river?" asked Basho.

"Oh, yes, of course, Master Basho!" one of the men said. "We would be most honored to carry you in our humble boat!"

"Thank you," said Basho.

Jack and Annie followed Basho onto the deck of the boat and sat next to the wicker baskets.

One of the fishermen untied the boat, and the others used long poles to push it away from the dock. The men began poling down the river.

The fishing boat floated under a series of bridges, moving in and out of shadows and glittering light. As it passed under one of the

bridges, it scraped the bottom of the river. Basho, Jack, and Annie were thrown forward.

"Forgive us, Master!" one of the fishermen called to Basho. "The river is very shallow."

"There has been no rain for a long time," said another fisherman. "It is very worrisome to us."

"Yes, it worries me, too," said Basho.

"What's everyone so worried about?" Annie asked Basho.

"When the weather is very dry, the people of Edo worry about fire," said Basho. "Twenty-five years ago, during a dry spell, half our city was destroyed by a terrible fire. Thousands died."

"Oh, that's awful!" said Annie.

"Yes. Since then, everyone has worked hard to rebuild the capital," said Basho. "Edo is now even more beautiful than before. In fact, along this riverbank are many new castles of the samurai. See? There one hides now."

Basho pointed at a steep rocky cliff above the riverbank. Jack shaded his eyes as he looked at the curved roof and high stone walls of a samurai castle. "Its largest room is called the Thousand-Mat Hall," said Basho.

"What does that mean?" asked Jack.

"It means the room can hold a thousand floor mats," said Basho.

"Cool," said Annie. "Basho, where do *you* live?"

Basho smiled. "My castle is on the other side of the Great Bridge," he said.

Jack wondered how many mats Basho's castle could hold.

Beyond the steep cliffs, the boat traffic grew heavier. Now there were many boats floating on the wide river: big sailboats, barges loaded with lumber, and ferries filled with passengers holding parasols.

The fishing boat glided toward a crowded dock next to a market. In the market, thousands of gleaming fish were laid out on tables. Men and women also sold fish and other sea creatures from baskets that hung from poles across their shoulders. "Shrimp!" "Tuna!" "Octopus!" "Eel!" they shouted.

"Wait for us while we deliver the fish," Basho said to Jack and Annie. "Then we will travel further on the river."

The fishermen tied up the boat. Jack and Annie waited on the landing as Basho helped the crew unload the wicker baskets. Then each man put a basket on his head and started up the stone steps that led to the fish market.

"Oh, no!" said Annie. "Look!" She pointed toward the other end of the dock.

Jack looked. He saw several samurai getting off a boat. "Quick! Grab a basket!" he said.

Jack and Annie each picked up a basket of fish. As Jack tried to lift the basket to his head, he tilted it. A couple of fish hit him on the nose as they fell to the dock.

"Leave them! Come on!" whispered Annie.

Carrying the baskets on their heads, Jack and Annie followed Basho and the fishermen up the steps and delivered their fish to a young woman at one of the tables. Jack glanced back at the river. The samurai were standing on the landing, checking someone's passport.

Jack looked at Basho. Basho was watching the samurai, too. He turned to the fishermen. "Thank you for the ride," he said calmly, bowing to the men. "We will walk from here."

The fishermen nodded and smiled.

Good plan, Jack thought, relieved.

"Come," said Basho. He led Jack and Annie away from the market. Soon they came to a busy road crowded with pedestrians and travelers on horseback.

As they walked along with the crowd, Jack remembered Basho's words: "Seek harmony with your surroundings." He tried to blend in by walking at a steady pace. Keeping his eyes down, he worried about their mission. *How will we ever find the secret of happiness*, he wondered, *if we have to keep dodging the samurai?*

"Look at that bridge!" said Annie.

Jack glanced up. A high, arched bridge spanned the river. Hundreds of people were walking across it.

"That is the Great Bridge," said Basho. "It will lead us away from the heart of Edo to the bank of the Sumida River, where I live."

"Great," said Jack. He hoped they would be safer away from the heart of Edo. Then maybe they could focus on their search for the secret.

Jack, Annie, and Basho joined the crowd crossing the bridge. They walked single file, close to the wooden railing. Jack stared straight ahead, careful not to look anyone in the eye. He saw people having picnics on the other side of the bridge. Kids were flying red kites.

"What's that mountain?" said Annie. She pointed to a snowcapped mountain looming in the distance. The white cone of the gray mountain rose above fleecy, rose-tinted clouds.

"That is a volcanic mountain called Mount Fuji," said Basho.

"Oh, I've heard of Mount Fuji!" said Jack. "That's the highest mountain in Japan, right?"

"Yes, and the most beautiful," said Basho.

"It *is* beautiful," said Annie.

Jack looked around. Actually, he thought everything seemed beautiful at that moment: the green and yellow parasols of the ferryboat passengers below, the pink cherry trees shimmering at the river's edge, the red kites and white seagulls gliding through the sky.

"I love Japan," Jack said softly.

"I do, too," said Basho. "We call our world 'the floating world,' for it seems to float on beauty."

"It really does," murmured Jack. Walking across the Great Bridge, he felt as if he himself were floating through the floating world.

CHAPTER FOUR

Sushi and Sumo

Basho led Jack and Annie off the Great Bridge and down a crowded road. They passed huge stacks of lumber. Then they came to a row of stages built along the riverbank. On one stage women were dancing. Their faces were painted white. They wore shimmering kimonos and waved fans.

Musicians played on a second stage. They plucked three-stringed instruments and blew on bamboo flutes. Their music was high-pitched and strange, but Jack liked it.

On another stage was a puppet show. Puppeteers wearing black clothes moved a giant dragon puppet around the stage. A man stood to the side and told a story to the audience. From the back of the crowd, it was hard to hear him.

"What's he saying?" said Annie.

"He is telling the legend of the Cloud Dragon," said Basho. "The Cloud Dragon is one of the guardian animals of the four directions. She has the power of flight and commands the rain clouds."

"Cool," said Annie.

Basho led them on past rows of stalls where craftspeople sold beads, cloth, kites, and paper lanterns. Some boys were holding up yo-yos for sale. Jack was surprised to see yo-yos in old Japan.

Beyond the craft stalls was a row of inns and cafés. The smell of spices and grilled fish filled the air.

"Yum," said Annie.

Jack was hungry, too.

"Would you like to stop at a teahouse?" Basho asked them.

"Yes!" Jack and Annie said together.

Basho led them toward a small building with an open front. At the entrance, Basho slipped off his sandals. Jack and Annie did the same. They placed their sandals in a row of shoes that other people had left by the door.

Inside the teahouse, cooks stirred steaming pots over a wood-burning stove. People sat at long low tables, eating with chopsticks and drinking from small cups. Several customers smiled shyly and bowed before Basho.

Basho must be a really famous teacher of the samurai, thought Jack. It made Jack feel important to be with him.

Basho led them to a table and sat cross-legged on a straw mat. Jack and Annie did the same. A waiter with a kerchief around his head hurried to the table. "Welcome to our humble teahouse, Master Basho!" he said.

"Thank you," said Basho.

Everyone is so polite in Japan! Jack thought.

The waiter handed Jack, Annie, and Basho warm wet towels. "Thank you," said Jack and Annie.

Jack watched Basho wipe his hands on the towel. He and Annie did the same. Then they all gave their towels back to the waiter.

"I would like plates of sushi for me and my two students, please," said Basho.

"Thank you," said the waiter, bowing.

While they waited for their food, Jack studied the people in the room. Jack noticed that even little kids were eating with chopsticks. He and

Annie had never had much luck using chopsticks in Asian restaurants back home.

Soon the waiter brought over three plates of small cakes of sticky rice wrapped in dark green, paper-like strips. He also brought napkins and three pairs of chopsticks.

When the waiter had gone, Basho spoke to Jack and Annie in a soft voice so no one else could hear. "We call this *sushi*," he said. "It is rice with pieces of raw fish in the middle."

"Raw fish?" said Jack. He gulped.

"And what's this part?" Annie pointed at the papery wrapping.

"Seaweed," said Basho.

"Seaweed?" said Jack.

"It is very good," said Basho.

Jack was so hungry he was willing to try anything, even raw fish and seaweed. His only problem was the chopsticks.

"Try it this way, Jack," said Annie. She carefully picked up a piece of sushi between the wooden ends of her chopsticks. Jack copied her. But as they both tried to bring their food to their mouths, their pieces of sushi fell onto the table.

Jack and Annie laughed and tried a second time. Annie was successful. But Jack dropped his sushi again. Without thinking, he grabbed it with his fingers and popped it into his mouth.

"Mmm!" said Jack. The vinegar-tasting rice, the raw fish, and the green, salty seaweed were delicious!

But Jack stopped in mid-chew. Two samurai at another table were glaring at him. One of the men had a big scar on his face. The other had fierce dark eyes.

Jack's throat was dry as he swallowed. *They saw me mess up with my chopsticks!* he thought. *They can tell I'm not from Japan!* He picked up another piece of sushi with his chopsticks. He glanced again at the samurai. They were watching him like hawks.

Jack's hand felt shaky. He tried to stay calm. He remembered a passage from their research book: *Samurai did not show their feelings. They had great powers of concentration.*

Jack tried very hard not to show his fear. He

concentrated on holding the sushi with his chopsticks. He raised the sushi to his mouth and ate it calmly. He lowered his chopsticks and picked up another piece of sushi. He ate it calmly.

When Jack looked back at the samurai, they were no longer watching him. Jack let out his breath. He picked up his last piece of sushi with his chopsticks and ate it calmly.

"Very good," said Basho, smiling at him.

"Thanks," said Jack.

"Let us go now," said Basho.

Basho folded his napkin neatly and left it beside his plate. Jack and Annie did the same. Basho paid for their meals, and then they stopped at the entranceway to put on their shoes. As they stepped outside, a drum began beating loudly. A huge crowd had gathered on the grassy riverbank.

"What's happening?" Annie asked.

"Come, I will show you," said Basho.

People moved aside so Basho could lead Jack and Annie to the front of the crowd.

A large ring had been marked off on the
ground with straw. In the middle of the circle,

two enormously fat men squatted at opposite
sides of the ring. Each man looked as if he

weighed more than four hundred pounds. They clapped their hands. Then each began stomping his feet.

"Who are *they*?" said Annie, her eyes wide.

"Sumo wrestlers," said Basho. "Sumo wrestling has been our most popular sport for over a thousand years."

The two wrestlers were now perfectly still. Crouching down with clenched fists, they were glaring at one another. The whole crowd seemed to hold its breath as the wrestlers stared into each other's eyes. Suddenly one wrestler lunged forward and grabbed the other. Then the hugely fat men began pushing each other around.

"They are trying to force each other out of the ring," said Basho.

Grunting and groaning, the two men moved backward and forward as spectators cheered wildly. Then one wrestler made a quick move and shoved his rival out of the circle. The crowd roared. Jack found himself cheering, too.

When the noise died down, Basho turned to Jack and Annie. "The first match is over," he said. "Shall we go now?"

Before Jack and Annie could answer him, two samurai stepped in front of them. One had a big scar on his face. The other had fierce dark eyes.

"Excuse me," the scar-faced man said. "May we see your passports, please?"

CHAPTER FIVE

An Excellent Student?

Jack froze.

Basho stepped forward. When the two samurai saw him, they bowed. "Good afternoon, Master," one said.

"Good afternoon," said Basho. "These are my students, Koto and Baku. I am afraid they left their passports at home today."

"They are your students?" said the samurai with the scar.

"Yes, excellent students," said Basho. "They have much natural talent."

"Ah." The two samurai looked at Jack and Annie with interest. "Will you share your talent with us?" one asked, smiling.

What talent? Jack wondered frantically. *Some samurai-warrior talent?*

Basho saw Jack's confusion. "Perhaps you would each recite one of your poems," he said.

"One of our poems?" squeaked Jack. *What kind of samurai talent is that?* he wondered. *Do samurai warriors have to know poems?*

"Sure," said Annie. "Here's a poem." She took a deep breath and then recited:

> *Twinkle, twinkle, little star,*
> *How I wonder what you are.*
> *Up above the world so high,*
> *Like a diamond in the sky.*

The samurai with the scar nodded. "Very good, Koto," he said. "The little star twinkles like a diamond."

The other samurai closed his eyes as if he

were seeing the star. "Yes, yes, very good!" he said. "A sparkling diamond high above the world! Excellent."

Both samurai then turned to Jack. "And you, Baku?" one said.

Jack stared at them. He couldn't remember *any* poem—not even a nursery rhyme!

"Uh . . . a poem? Right," said Jack. "Um. Let's see. . . . Okay." He took a deep breath and said:

> *I love Japan.*
> *Oh, man.*
> *I really love Japan.*
> *The land of Japan*
> *Is cool.*

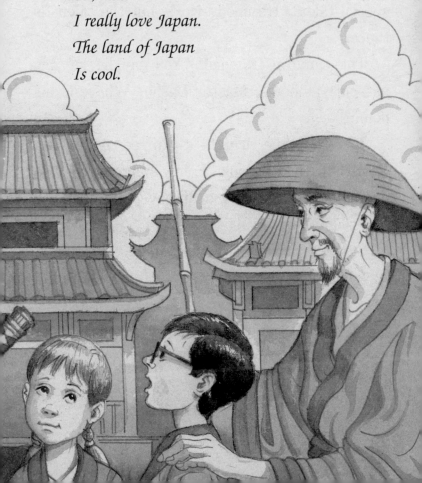

Jack bit his lip. He knew his poem was bad. He glanced at Annie. She looked as if she were trying not to laugh.

The dark-eyed samurai turned to Basho. "An excellent student?" he said.

Basho nodded. "Well, yes. . . . Baku has a—a special talent. He needs work, but the talent is there."

The samurai frowned. "You say he left his passport at home, Master Basho? Where is his home?"

Just then the drumbeat started again. The samurai turned to look. A new sumo match was beginning. The two samurai moved closer to the ring to get a better look.

Basho turned to Jack and Annie. "We should leave now," he said calmly. "I will take you to my home, where you will be safe."

Jack, Annie, and Basho quickly left the sumo crowd and blended in with shoppers walking down a busy street. Peddlers carried long poles over their shoulders with baskets swinging on the ends. They shouted about their wares: "Shoes and socks!" "Cakes and pastries!" "Rope and twine!"

One woman had a large box strapped to her back. "Books! Books!" she shouted.

"No thank you," said Jack. He loved books, but he kept going. He was afraid the samurai might show up again at any moment.

A boy carried birdcages and shouted, "Birds! Birds!"

Suddenly Jack felt a hand on his shoulder. He nearly had a heart attack! But it was just Basho. "I live *that* way," said Basho, pointing. "Over the bridge."

Jack and Annie walked with Basho over a small, narrow bridge that crossed a canal.

Basho led them past a temple, then past small bamboo houses with chickens in their yards. Little children were spinning tops on the dusty ground. One called out, "Hello, Master Basho!" Basho smiled and waved.

Then Jack and Annie walked with Basho along the dirt path bordering the river. Tall pine trees lined the riverbank. A dry wind blew leaves and pine needles into the shallows. Jack started to breathe more easily. He felt safer now.

The trail grew more narrow. The sun slipped behind the tops of the trees. Jack was eager to get to Basho's castle. He looked for a steep roof and high stone walls like the castles of the samurai.

Through the deepening shadows of twilight, Basho led them to a clearing not far from the river.

At the center of the clearing was a pond overgrown with weeds. On the far side of the pond, moss-covered stones led to the door of a tiny hut. The hut was made of bamboo and had a roof of wood shingles. Next to the small hut was a large plant with droopy green leaves.

"Welcome to my castle," said Basho.

CHAPTER SIX

The Banana Tree

"*This* is your castle?" said Jack.

Basho smiled. "In my heart, my humble cottage is grander than all the castles of the samurai," he explained. "And my banana tree is more beautiful to me than all the beauty of the Imperial Garden."

Jack and Annie stared at the large plant with the long, droopy leaves.

"I like this tree so much I have taken my name from it," said Basho. "*Basho* means 'banana tree.'"

"Cool," said Annie. She looked around. "It's nice here."

Not really, thought Jack. The cottage was shabby and the droopy banana tree looked scrawny and sad to him.

"Please come inside," said Basho. He slipped off his sandals and left them outside. He picked

up a bundle of wood, then ducked through the low door that led into his hut.

Jack and Annie took off their shoes, too, and followed Basho into a small, shadowy room.

Basho opened his shutters to let in the evening air. "Please sit," he said.

"Thank you," said Jack and Annie. Jack looked around the room for chairs, but there

weren't any. The only furniture was a low wooden table and a bamboo chest. Three straw mats covered the earthen floor. Jack and Annie sat down on one of the mats.

Basho lit a small oil lamp. Then he made a fire in his fireplace. "I will prepare tea for us," he said. "Rest while I draw water from the river." He picked up one of the two wooden buckets near the door and headed outside.

When Basho was gone, Jack and Annie looked at each other. "I guess this is a three-mat house," said Annie.

Jack nodded. "You'd think a famous teacher of the samurai would have a hundred-mat house . . . or at least a fifty-mat house," he said.

"I like this house, though," said Annie. "It's cozy."

"I wonder who Basho is exactly," said Jack.

"If he's famous, maybe he's in our book," said Annie. "Look him up."

"Good idea," said Jack. He pulled the research

book out of his bag. By the light of the crackling fire, he looked up *Basho* in the index. "He *is* here!" Jack turned to the right page and read aloud.

Basho is one of Japan's greatest poets. He wrote short, beautiful poems that speak to people as clearly today as they did during the Edo period of Japan.

"Basho's a great *poet*!" said Annie. "That explains everything!"

"Sort of . . . ," said Jack. "It explains why we had to recite poems to the samurai. But it doesn't explain why Basho lives in such a dinky house."

Basho opened the door and came in with his bucket. Jack closed the book and slipped it back into his bag.

Basho poured river water into an iron pot over the fire. He pulled three tiny bowls and a small cloth bag from the bamboo chest. He took loose green tea from the bag and dropped it into the bowls. Then he waited patiently for the water to boil.

Jack and Annie waited patiently, too. Listening to the soft rushing sounds of the river outside, Jack started to feel peaceful for the first time all day.

When the water was hot, Basho poured some into each of the tea bowls. Then he handed the warm bowls to Annie and Jack.

"Thank you," said Annie.

"Thank you," said Jack.

"You are welcome," said Basho.

Jack carefully took a sip from the steaming bowl. The green tea tasted bitter, but he didn't mind it.

"Hmm, interesting taste," said Annie. "Basho, Jack was wondering, if you're a famous poet, why do you live in such a dinky house?"

"Annie!" said Jack, embarrassed. "She's kidding. I wasn't really wondering that."

Basho laughed. "Long ago, I trained to be a samurai," he said. "But I was not happy. All I wanted to do was write poetry. A poet does not need to live in a castle. A poet needs to live with the wind and the clouds, the flowers and the birds. Here, I have a small garden and my banana tree. I have the sound of the river all day long. Here, I have everything I need to write my poems."

"What do you write about?" asked Annie.

"Small things," said Basho. "A crow picking snails out of the mud, a woodpecker hammering a tree, pine needles scattered by the wind. A poet finds beauty in all the small things of nature."

"And you teach poetry to the samurai?" asked Jack.

"Yes, the samurai greatly honor the art of poetry," said Basho. "Poetry helps focus the mind. The samurai believe a truly brave warrior should be able to compose a poem even in the midst of an earthquake, or while facing an enemy on the battlefield."

"Can you say one of your poems for us?" asked Annie.

"Let me think," said Basho. "Well . . . I was working on a new poem yesterday." He reached for a wooden box under the table. He took a small piece of delicate paper from the box and read aloud:

> *An old pond:*
> *a frog jumps in—*
> *the sound of water.*

Basho looked up at Jack and Annie.

"Hmm," said Jack. "Nice beginning."

"It is not just the beginning," said Basho. "It is the whole poem. A small moment in time."

"I think it's great," said Annie. "I love frogs. Your poem makes me love them even more."

"Would you read it again, please?" Jack said. He felt like he must have missed something.

Basho read again:

> *An old pond:*
> *a frog jumps in—*
> *the sound of water.*

Jack nodded thoughtfully. "Good," he said. "It's really good." And he meant it. The poem made him feel as if he himself had been right there, by that pond, hearing the frog splash into the water, breaking the silence.

"If you like it, you may have it," said Basho. He handed the paper to Jack.

"Thanks!" said Jack. As he put the poem in his bag, a bell rang softly in the distance.

"Ah, the temple bells," said Basho. He stood up. "It is time to rest. I will take a mat and sleep outside. I enjoy sleeping under the stars. And now, because of the poem you recited today, Annie, I shall think of them as diamonds in the sky."

Annie smiled.

"You can stay inside and cover yourselves with these mosquito nets," said Basho. He pulled some nets from the bamboo chest and handed them to Jack and Annie. "But do not worry, in my small house there are only small mosquitoes—not giant ones like those in the Imperial Palace."

Jack and Annie laughed at Basho's joke. He gave a net to each of them. Then he picked up one of the mats from the floor and pulled it outside, closing the door behind him.

The fire in the fireplace had died down. The light from the oil lamp had nearly gone out, too. Jack and Annie lay on the straw mats and covered themselves with the mosquito nets. A cricket chirped on the hearth. Jack noticed a patch of light on the floor. He realized it was moonlight coming through the open window.

Jack reached out from under the net and put his hand on the square of pale moonlight. He could hear the rustling of the banana plant in the breeze. Half asleep, he imagined himself swaying with its long, broad leaves.

"This dinky hut is much nicer than a castle," Annie murmured. "I feel like we're tiny crickets going to sleep."

"Yeah . . . I feel like I'm holding moonlight in my hand," said Jack, "and like I'm a banana leaf . . . dancing in the wind."

"Sounds like a poem," said Annie.

"Yeah . . . maybe I should write it down . . . ," said Jack. But instead, he fell fast asleep.

CHAPTER SEVEN

Clang, Clang, Clang!

Clang, clang, clang!

Jack opened his eyes. The sound of bells filled the night—not the gentle ringing of the temple bells but a harsh clanging.

Jack smelled smoke. He and Annie threw off their mosquito nets and stumbled to the door.

Basho was standing in his yard, looking at the dawn sky. It was black with smoke. The bells kept clanging.

"Is there a fire?" asked Jack.

"Yes," said Basho. "It must be very big, for

the bells do not stop ringing from the watch-tower. This is what we have feared most. I must go and help the firefighters."

"We'll help, too," said Jack.

"No, stay here," said Basho. He pulled on his socks and sandals, then grabbed a wooden bucket by the door. "If the fire gets close, wade into the river, where you will be safe."

"But we want to help!" said Annie.

"Yes, wait for us!" said Jack. He and Annie pulled on their socks and sandals.

"Come, then," said Basho. "But if the fire begins to spread, you must promise to return here to the river."

"We promise!" said Annie.

"Then bring the other bucket and follow me," said Basho.

"I'll get it," said Jack. He hurried into the hut and grabbed the wooden bucket by the hearth. It was heavy, even without water in it. Jack hugged the bucket to his chest and rushed back outside.

Jack and Annie followed Basho through the pine forest. They passed a farmhouse where two small children stood outside, looking at the fiery sky.

"Our father says the lumberyard near the river is burning!" the boy shouted to Basho.

"He has gone to help fight the fire!" said the girl. "Great piles of wood are burning!"

The fire bells kept clanging as Basho, Jack, and Annie rushed past the temple and across the narrow footbridge.

They hurried up the winding dirt path until they came to the shopping market. In the smoky red dawn, people were pushing carts piled high with goods. They were running away from the fire.

But Basho, Jack, and Annie ran *toward* the fire. The air grew hotter and smokier near the teahouses and the performance stages. Sparks flew through the sky. Tiles on rooftops were catching fire and crashing to the ground.

Basho led Jack and Annie farther through the smoke until they came to the lumberyard. The fire roared as it burned piles of logs. Flames rose high into the sky.

Firefighters were passing buckets of water up a line from the river to the fire. Others waved huge fans to beat back the windblown flames,

while the most daring worked with hooks and axes, trying to separate the burning timber.

"Help the bucket brigade!" Basho said to Jack and Annie. "Get water from the river!"

Basho rushed to help the men beating back the fire with fans while Jack and Annie hurried down to the river. Jack filled their wooden

bucket. With water inside, it was so heavy he couldn't lift it.

"Do it together!" said Annie.

"Right!" said Jack.

Using all their strength, Jack and Annie carried their bucket up the bank of the river. As they stumbled along, they tried not to spill the water. Jack could hardly breathe in the smoke-filled air. His throat and eyes burned. His face felt red-hot. Finally, when he thought he couldn't take another step, they got to the bucket brigade. They gave their bucket to the person at the end, who gave them an empty bucket. "Get more!" he said.

Jack and Annie hurried back to the river with the empty bucket. They filled it with water and then struggled back up the bank.

Over and over, Jack and Annie hauled buckets of water back and forth from the river to the line of firefighters. Everyone worked hard to battle the great blaze. But the flames kept shooting into the sky. Eventually the fire leapt over the river, and timber on the far bank began to burn.

"Oh, no!" cried a woman. "All of Edo will catch fire now!"

"The rice-storage houses will burn down!" said a man. "The harvest will be destroyed!"

Several people began weeping. Jack felt like crying, too. Right in front of his eyes, the beautiful floating world of Edo was about to go up in flames. "This is hopeless!" he said to Annie.

"No, it's not!" Annie said. "The wand! We can use the wand!"

"Of course!" cried Jack. "But it's in my bag! Back at Basho's house!"

"We have to get it!" said Annie. She shouted to Basho, "Basho, we're going back to your castle!"

"Yes, run for safety!" called Basho. "Jump into the river!"

"Right!" cried Jack.

"Be careful!" Annie shouted to Basho. Then

she and Jack started running as fast as they could. They raced past the market. They ran across the footbridge, past the temple and the farmhouse, and through the grove of pines to Basho's house.

Jack and Annie ran inside the tiny hut. Jack grabbed his bag and pulled out the wand. He waved it through the air. "Do something to make the fire stop!" he shouted.

Jack held his breath and waited.

"Let me try!" said Annie. She took the wand and waved it. "Stop the fire over Edo *now*!" she shouted.

Jack and Annie waited again.

"It's not working!" cried Jack. "We must be doing something wrong."

"But this is for the good of everyone!" said Annie.

"I know, I know!" said Jack.

"And we've tried our hardest!" said Annie. "Everybody has!"

"Five words!" said Jack. "We have to use five words!"

"Oh, right!" said Annie. She waved the wand through the air again. "Put. Out. The. Fire!" she yelled.

"One more word!" cried Jack.

"Please!" shouted Annie.

Jack and Annie were blasted by a blinding light. Jack felt himself shooting through brightness, then darkness, then back into light. An icy wind blew. The air was crystal-clear. Early sunlight flashed on rock.

Jack and Annie were standing on the ledge of a mountain.

CHAPTER EIGHT

In the Red Dawn

"Are you—are you okay?" Annie asked Jack. She was still holding the wand. Her pigtails blew in the bright wind.

"Yeah, yeah, but what happened?" said Jack in a daze. He was freezing and out of breath. "Where are we?"

"I don't know," whispered Annie.

Jack shielded his eyes from the brilliant light of the red dawn and looked around. Pink clouds floated through the air like piles of cotton candy. Through a gap in the clouds, he saw hills shrouded in black smoke below. Beneath the smoke, flames rose from the city of Edo.

"I think we're on Mount Fuji," said Annie.

"Mount Fuji?" said Jack. "That's crazy! Why are we *here*?" He stopped to catch his breath. He felt dizzy and light-headed. "Edo's burning! We should be *there*!"

"Maybe the wand didn't understand," said Annie. "Maybe it was trying to save us by taking us far away from the fire."

Suddenly a great mass of thick clouds piled up, ringing the mountaintop like a wall. The clouds swirled and whirled and tumbled. They changed color, from rose to gold to gray to white.

"What's going on?" cried Jack.

The head of a gigantic monster rose from the bubbling clouds!

"AHHH!" Jack and Annie screamed. They grabbed each other and crouched down on the rocky ledge.

The monster had spiky eyebrows and long, curled whiskers. It had the horns of a deer, the forked tongue of a snake, and the fiery breath of a dragon. Through the swirling clouds, Jack and Annie could see the dragon's snake-like body curling through the clouds and down the mountainside. Its back was covered with shiny scales. Its spine had a row of shark-like fins.

The dragon reached out its claws. They were like the claws of an eagle—only a thousand times bigger! The claws gripped the side of the mountain.

Jack made himself as small as he could. He covered his head. But Annie jumped to her feet. "I get it!" she cried. "I know what's happening! Thank you for coming!"

"Annie, get down!" Jack shouted.

"Jack, it's the Cloud Dragon!" said Annie. "The puppet show—remember? The wand sent her here!"

"What? Why?" cried Jack.

"She makes rain! Don't you remember? Rain!" cried Annie. *"She commands the rain clouds!"*

The dragon lowered her giant head, stretching it over the mountain ledge. Her scales glittered honey-gold in the dawn light. She was still, very still, as if she were waiting for something.

"Come on! We have to climb on her back!" shouted Annie.

"Why?" cried Jack.

"We have to go with her!" said Annie. "The wand brought us to the dragon! Now it's up to us to show her what to do!"

"Okay! Okay!" said Jack.

Annie climbed onto the back of the Cloud Dragon. She sat between two of the dragon's shark-like fins. Jack climbed on behind her. He gripped the fin in front of him as if he were holding on to the horn of a saddle.

"Fly over the fire!" yelled Annie. "Make rain!"

"Lots of it!" shouted Jack.

The Cloud Dragon slid off the mountain ledge.

Jack trembled with cold as the monster slithered through the freezing sea of clouds, like a snake through the grass.

Above Edo, Jack looked down. Billowing black smoke and red flames shot into the dawn sky.

"Now! Rain now!" Jack said.

The Cloud Dragon reared back her head. Great black clouds flowed from her mouth. The clouds spread across the sky. There was a crack of thunder and a flash of lightning. Then rain began to pour down on the city.

The dragon twisted her head this way and that. More clouds blew from her mouth, and more rain fell on the burning city of Edo.

As the dragon slithered through the sky, breathing out mountains of storm clouds, rain fell
on the flat lands of the rice fields,
on the Imperial Garden,
the samurai castles,
the fish market,
and the Great Bridge.

Rain fell on the floating world of inns and stages, teahouses, temples, and farms.

Rain fell on the lumberyard and the pine forest and the canals.

Slowly the rain washed away all the smoke and flames. Even after the fires of Edo no longer flickered, the Cloud Dragon breathed more black clouds, and the rain kept falling, falling steadily, soaking the gardens and fields, filling the shallow rivers and dried-up ponds.

"The fire's out!" Jack shouted.

"Take us to Basho's!" Annie yelled to the dragon.

The Cloud Dragon twisted her giant body. She slid through the dark clouds. Then she reared up—until Jack and Annie couldn't hold on any longer and they were falling backward, somersaulting through the air!

SPLASH! SPLASH!

Jack sank to the bottom of the river. He flailed his arms and struggled to the surface. His head bobbed up—he spewed out water and gasped for air. He had lost his glasses. He dove back down and grabbed them from the river bottom, then swam back to the surface. Treading water, he wiped his glasses, then put them on.

"Hi!" Annie yelled. She was holding the wand in the air, above the water.

"Hi!" Jack yelled back.

Jack and Annie swam toward the bank of the river. They swam until their feet could touch bottom. Then they dragged themselves out of the water and collapsed on the muddy bank.

They had lost their socks and sandals. Their silk kimonos clung to their bodies. Dripping wet, they gasped for breath and looked up at the sky.

Big drops of rain splashed on their faces. There was no sign of the Cloud Dragon. But the cool rain kept falling, bathing the floating world of Edo.

CHAPTER NINE

Flowers of Edo

"We did it!" said Annie. "We made our own magic!"

"Yeah, we got the Cloud Dragon to put out the fire," breathed Jack. He felt dazed. "Do you think we're near Basho's house?"

"I think so," said Annie. "We asked the Cloud Dragon to take us there, so I bet she did. Come on, let's find Basho."

Jack and Annie stood up and started walking along the edge of the river. They walked barefoot through the mud, under dripping trees.

"Hey, there's the clearing," said Annie.

Jack and Annie headed toward the clearing beyond the trees and tall grass.

"Oh, no!" cried Annie. "Look!"

In the clearing, rain was falling on the charred ruins of Basho's house. The shingled roof and the bamboo walls of the little hut had burned and collapsed.

"Where's Basho?" said Jack, scared.

"There!" said Annie.

The famous poet sat on a log next to his banana tree in the gray rain. His clothes were blackened. His face was covered with soot. He clutched his writing box.

"Basho!" yelled Annie.

Basho looked up. A smile crossed his dirty, weathered face. "I looked for you by the river, but didn't see you!" he said. "I am glad you are safe."

"We're glad you're safe, too," said Jack.

"But your castle! Your castle burned down," said Annie.

"Yes. It burned before the miracle of the rain," said Basho, sighing.

Jack and Annie sat on the log next to him. Through the smoky drizzle, they all stared at the rubble. Trees and plants dripped with rain. A pigeon cooed.

For a long moment, no one spoke. Then Annie broke the silence. "I'm glad you still have your banana tree," she said. "I like the sound of the rain falling on the leaves."

Basho looked up, but didn't say anything.

"Yeah, and I like the sound of the river," said Jack. "It's louder now since the rain came."

Basho tilted his head as if listening to the rain on the leaves of the banana plant and to the steady rushing sounds of the river. His face softened. "Yes, I like those things, too," he said. He held up his wooden box. "And I still have my poems."

"Don't worry, Basho," said Annie. "Everything can be built again."

"And your castle will be even more beautiful than before," said Jack.

Basho smiled. "I suppose that is why the ancients called our fires 'the flowers of Edo,'" he said.

"What do you mean?" asked Jack.

"After something is destroyed by fire, a good new thing often takes its place," said Basho. "Just as after the bleakest winter, beautiful flowers return with the spring."

"I'm sure you'll make many beautiful flowers," said Annie.

"Thank you," said Basho. "I am sorry, though, that you and Jack will not have a place to stay now."

"Don't worry," said Annie. "We have to travel back to our own house."

"How far away is that?" asked Basho.

"*Very* far," said Annie. She and Jack stood up. "But we just need to get back to the Imperial Garden. We'll know the way from there."

"Good," said Basho. He stood up. "Come, I will accompany you back to the garden."

"Thanks, that would be great!" said Jack.

Basho picked up his walking stick. Then he led Jack and Annie along the bank of the river. Through the light drizzle, they saw a ferryboat moving upstream. Basho waved, and the pilot steered the boat to shore.

Jack and Annie followed Basho onto the ferry. The three of them sat together on a wooden bench. The other passengers stared at them. Many had ashes on their clothes and soot on their faces. Jack was relieved to see that no samurai were on board.

"Greetings, Master Basho," the pilot said. The other passengers nodded respectfully to Basho. They smiled as if the presence of the great poet gave them hope.

"The rains were a miracle, were they not, Master Basho?" an old woman said.

"Indeed they were," said Basho.

"I guess the Cloud Dragon showed up just in time," said Annie.

"*Annie*," whispered Jack.

Basho smiled at her. "I am afraid no one believes in the Cloud Dragon anymore, Annie," he said. "But it is lovely to pretend, is it not?"

"Yes, it is lovely," said Annie.

The rain stopped as the ferryboat traveled on up the river. Mist rose from the water, and birds began to sing.

When they passed the teahouses, Jack and Annie saw firefighters cleaning up after the fire, sweeping up broken tiles and scrubbing the walkways. Waiters were bringing them tea.

The sun was shining by the time they passed the puppet stage and the charred lumberyard. Wisps of smoke still rose from the black piles of burned logs.

The ferryboat floated on through the bright morning. It glided under the Great Bridge and past the crowded fish market. Fishermen were hauling in their catch from the night before.

By the time they moved past the samurai castles and came near the moat of the Imperial

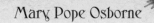

Garden, the sun had completely dried out Jack's and Annie's kimonos.

The boat pulled up to the landing. Basho helped Jack and Annie onto the dock. He waved good-bye to the boat passengers.

Jack, Annie, and Basho walked over the stone bridge that crossed the moat. They walked through the massive gate in the high wall. Then they followed the paths of the Imperial Garden, around the big rocks and the pond with the swans.

Jack kept an eye out for horses and samurai warriors. But the garden was as peaceful as when they had first landed. It was filled with birdsong. The willows swayed. Water from the waterfall tumbled into the green pool. Jack caught sight of the sun shining on the tree house high in the cherry tree.

Jack stopped walking. "We know our way home from here," he said to Basho.

"Are you certain?" asked Basho. He did not seem to notice the tree house in the cherry tree.

"We're sure," said Annie. "Once we start on our way, the trip will be easy."

Basho nodded. "You remind me of the famous saying of the samurai Musashi," he said. "'*A journey of a thousand miles begins with one step.*'"

"I've heard that saying before," said Jack.

"Words can outlive their creators," said Basho. "Though I will never be so lucky as to have mine outlive me."

"Don't be too sure of that," said Annie.

Basho gave them a little smile. "I hope you both will return to Edo someday," he said. "Look for me when you come back. I should have a lovely new castle on the river by then."

"Thanks," said Jack.

"Good-bye," said Annie.

They both bowed to Basho.

Basho bowed to them. Then the great poet turned and left them. Falling cherry blossoms floated on the wind as he walked away.

Jack and Annie watched Basho until they could no longer see him. Then they turned to go. Just as they started walking, a man stepped out from the shadows of the garden. The man wore a blue coat and two swords hung from his belt.

"Excuse me," said the samurai. "May I see your passports, please?"

CHAPTER TEN

Journey of a Thousand Miles

Jack couldn't speak.

"Our passports?" said Annie. "They—um—they got destroyed in a fire—on the other side of the Great Bridge."

The samurai narrowed his eyes. "Your passports *burned*?" he said. "Why were you on the other side of the Great Bridge?"

"We were with Master Basho," said Jack.

"Master Basho?" said the samurai.

"Yes," said Annie. "We are students of his."

"Ah!" The samurai's expression brightened.

"So you study poetry with Master Basho?"

"Yes," said Annie. "Would you like to hear some poems?"

Oh, no! thought Jack. *Not again!*

"Yes, please," said the samurai.

"No problem." Annie thought for a moment and then said: "Here's a simple little poem." She recited:

> *Rain falls outside,*
> *But the tiny cricket on the hearth*
> *Is dry tonight.*

The samurai nodded. "Hmm," he said. "Yes. Very simple, but very lovely."

"Thank you," said Annie.

The man turned to Jack. Jack could hardly breathe. His mind was blank. He looked to Annie for help. But Annie just smiled, waiting to hear his poem.

Jack cleared his throat. He tried to stay calm. He closed his eyes and let his mind roam over their visit to Japan. He opened his eyes. He looked up at the cloudless sky and said:

The sun is shining,
The day is hot.
But moonlight
And cool breezes
Still fill my heart,
Left over from last night.

"Whoa!" whispered Annie. "Good!"

"Yes, very good!" said the samurai. He looked at the sky. "The moonlight, the cool breeze," he mused, "left over from the night. Very good. Master Basho has taught you well!"

The samurai strolled away, shaking his head and murmuring to himself. He let out a happy laugh, as if delighted with the day.

Jack couldn't believe it. They were free! "Hurry, let's go," he said. "Before someone *else* sees us!"

Jack and Annie ran to the rope ladder and

started up. As soon as they climbed inside the tree house, Jack grabbed the Pennsylvania book. He found a picture of the Frog Creek woods. "As the famous samurai once said, 'A journey of a thousand miles begins with one step,'" said Jack.

"Or one *sentence*," said Annie.

"Right," said Jack. He pointed at the picture. "I wish we could go home."

Annie gasped. "Wait a minute!" she said. "We forgot our mission!"

"What?" said Jack.

But the wind started to blow.

The tree house started to spin.

It spun faster and faster.

Then everything was still.

Absolutely still.

The early-morning air was cold.

Jack and Annie were back in Frog Creek,

wearing their own clothes. Jack's burlap bag was a backpack again. He looked inside to make sure the Wand of Dianthus was there. It was. And Basho's frog poem was there, too.

"I can't believe it!" said Annie. "We didn't look for a secret of happiness for Merlin. How could we forget that?"

"Oh, man," said Jack. "We were so busy worrying about the samurai and putting out the fire that we forgot our mission."

"What will Morgan say?" said Annie. "We've *never* forgotten a mission before! And this one was the most important we've ever had! To help save Merlin!" Annie was near tears.

"Wait, wait. Calm down," said Jack. "Let's think a minute. Maybe we actually found a secret of happiness. Maybe we just don't know we found it."

"You mean, like—were we *extra* happy at any time?" asked Annie.

"Yeah, sort of," said Jack. "Were we?"

"I don't know, were you?" said Annie.

"I think a few times . . . ," said Jack.

"Like when?" said Annie.

"Like when we were crossing the Great Bridge with Basho, I felt sort of happy then," said Jack.

"Me too," said Annie. "And I was pretty happy eating sushi."

"Yeah, but I got scared when I saw the samurai watching me," said Jack.

"What about the sumo-wrestling match?" asked Annie.

"That was fun," said Jack. "But I don't know if it really made me *happy*."

"Riding the dragon and putting out the fire?" said Annie.

"That was great," said Jack. "But I was too worried about saving the city to be happy."

"Making up poems for the samurai?" said Annie.

"Too nervous," said Jack.

"Well, when were you *purely* happy?" said Annie.

"I think it was when . . ." Jack stopped. He felt silly saying what he was about to say.

"Go ahead," said Annie.

"I think it was when I was lying on the mat in Basho's house," said Jack, "and I touched that little patch of moonlight on the floor and I listened to the banana leaves in the wind."

"Oh, yes!" said Annie. "Before we fell asleep, and I heard the cricket and I felt like I was a cricket myself going to sleep in a cozy place."

"Yeah, like that," said Jack.

"It's like what Basho said about finding beauty in the small things of nature," said Annie, "like his poem about that frog splashing in the water."

"I think that's it!" said Jack. "A secret of happiness is paying really close attention to the small things in nature."

"Wow," said Annie. "I think that's a great secret to share with Merlin."

"It is," said Jack, "and Basho's poem will help Merlin understand."

"Right," said Annie.

"Let's go," said Jack.

Annie climbed down the rope ladder. Jack put his pack on his back and followed her.

As Jack and Annie started through the chilly woods together, Jack noticed things he hadn't seen before. He saw tiny blue wildflowers sprouting up from the winter-weary ground.

He saw fresh anthills in the dirt.

He saw leaf buds on twigs and green moss on a rock, bright in the March sunlight.

"I feel like I'm seeing spring for the first time," said Jack.

"Me too," said Annie.

"Not just for the first time this year," said Jack. "But for the first time in my whole life."

"Me too," said Annie.

Jack felt happy, *really* happy, as he and Annie headed for home in the sparkling morning light.

More About Basho, Edo, and Haiku

The poet **Basho** was born in Japan in 1644. His family wanted him to grow up to be a samurai. But when he was a young man, he decided to write poetry instead.

Basho was poor and unknown for many years. Gradually, though, people started to read his poetry and, over time, he became very famous! His poetry fans built him a small house near the river Sumida. A student gave him a banana tree—*basho*, in Japanese—to plant in his yard. In 1682, Basho's house was destroyed by a fire that swept through **Edo**. (Edo was often in danger from fires because the buildings were made of wood. As mentioned in this story, a terrible fire in 1657 had burned nearly all the city!)

A new house was built for Basho, but he did not live there for long. In 1684, he began the first of his journeys around Japan. Basho even wrote a book about his travels called *The Narrow Road to the Deep North*, in which he combined journal writing and poetry.

The form of poetry that Basho is famous for is called **haiku** (say HI-koo). It is the shortest form of Japanese poetry. Haiku poetry is written in plain speech and often describes humble things of everyday life. At first, haiku poetry seems very simple, but it can have a deep effect on a reader. A good haiku poem can waken your senses and help you see life in a fresh way—like it did for Jack, Annie, and the other people in this story.

Turn the page for great activities!

Fun Activities for Jack and Annie and *You*!

Write your own haiku!

As Jack and Annie found out in ancient Japan, anyone can be a poet! Haiku are simple but moving poems, often about nature or everyday life. Would you like to write one of your own? Get a pencil and give it a try!

Haiku are usually three lines long. Often the first line is five syllables long, the second line has seven syllables, and the third has five again. These are not strict rules, but they give an idea of how short a haiku really is.

Sit down and think about something you feel strongly about. It could be the beauty of the stars. It could be the comfort of a warm pair of mittens. Then write a simple three-line poem that makes people feel what you feel. That's your haiku!

Puzzle of the Red Dawn

Jack and Annie learned many new things on their adventure in ancient Japan. Did you?

Put your knowledge to the test with this puzzle. You can use a notebook or make a copy of this page if you don't want to write in your book.

1. Traditional huge wrestlers.

☐ ☐ ◯ ☐

2. An ancient Japanese military leader.

☐ ◯ ☐ ☐ ☐ ☐

3. A Japanese robe.

☐ ☐ ☐ ☐ ◯ ☐

4. Today's name for the Imperial City of Edo.

☐ ☐ ☐ ◯ ☐

5. Ancient Japanese warriors with a strict code.

☐ ☐ ☐ ☐ ◯ ☐ ☐

6. The Japanese word for banana tree.

☐ ◯ ☐ ☐ ☐

7. The legendary guardian animal that commands the rain clouds.

☐ ☐ ◯ ☐ ☐
☐ ☐ ☐ ☐ ☐ ☐

Now look at your answers above. The letters that are circled spell a word—but that word is scrambled! Can you unscramble it to spell a word that Jack and Annie try to achieve throughout their adventure in the Imperial City?

Here's a special preview of

Magic Tree House #38
(A Merlin Mission)
Monday with a Mad Genius

Jack and Annie go on another amazing
adventure filled with history, magic, and
even flight!

Now available in hardcover.
Paperback edition coming January 2009!

Excerpt copyright © 2007 by Mary Pope Osborne.
Published by Random House Children's Books.

CHAPTER ONE

Old Friends

Jack poured milk over his cereal. His stomach felt fluttery. It was Monday—the first day of a new school year.

Jack always felt nervous on the first day. What would his new teacher be like? Would his desk be close to a window? Would friends from last year be in his class again this year?

"Annie, hurry!" Jack's mom called upstairs. "It's fifteen minutes till eight. School starts in half an hour."

Jack's dad walked into the kitchen. "Are you

sure you and Annie don't want me to drive you?" he asked.

"No thanks, we don't mind walking," said Jack. Their school was only three blocks away.

"Annie, *hurry*!" their mom called again. "You're going to be late!"

The back door banged open. Annie rushed into the kitchen. She was out of breath.

"Oh, I thought you were upstairs," their mom said with surprise. "You were outside?"

"Yes!" said Annie, panting. "Just taking a quick walk." She looked at Jack. Her eyes sparkled. "Hurry, Jack. We really should go *now*!"

"Okay, I'm coming!" said Jack. He leapt up from the table. He could tell Annie wasn't talking about school. *The tree house must be back! Finally!*

Jack grabbed his backpack. Annie held the door open for him.

"No breakfast?" their mom asked.

"Too nervous to eat now, Mom," said Jack.

"Me too," said Annie. "Bye, Mom! Bye, Dad!"

"Have fun," their mom said.

"Learn a lot," said their dad.

"Don't worry, we will!" said Annie.

Jack and Annie slipped out the door and walked quickly across their yard.

"It's back!" said Annie.

"I figured it was!" said Jack.

"Morgan must want us to look for another secret of happiness to help Merlin," said Annie.

"Yep!" said Jack. "Let's run!"

Jack and Annie dashed up the sidewalk. They crossed the street and headed into the Frog Creek woods. They ran between the trees, through shadows and light, until they came to the tallest oak.

High in the tree was the magic tree house. The rope ladder was swaying in the chilly morning wind.

"How did you know it was here?" asked Jack, catching his breath.

"I woke up thinking about Teddy and Kathleen," said Annie, "and I had this strange feeling."

"Really?" said Jack. "Teddy! Kathleen!" he shouted up at the tree house.

Two young teenagers looked out the tree house window: a curly-haired boy with freckles and a big grin and a smiling girl with sea-blue eyes and dark wavy hair.

"Jack! Annie!" the girl said.

"Come up! Come up!" said the boy.

Jack and Annie hurried up the rope ladder. When they climbed inside the tree house, they threw their arms around their friends.

"Are we going to look for another secret of happiness?" said Annie. "To help Merlin?"

"Yes, and this time you will travel back to Florence, Italy, five hundred years ago," said Teddy.

"Florence, Italy?" said Jack. "What's there?"

"An amazing person who will help you," said Kathleen.

"Who?" asked Annie. "Is this person magical?"

Teddy grinned. "Some people might say so," he said. He reached into his cloak and pulled out a book. The cover showed a drawing of a man wearing a purple cloak and floppy blue cap. He had a long nose, bright, kind eyes with heavy eyebrows, and a flowing beard. The title said:

"Leonardo da Vinci!" said Jack. "Are you kidding?"

"I've heard of him," said Annie.

"Who hasn't?" said Jack. "He was an incredible genius!"

"This biography of Leonardo will help you on your mission," said Teddy.

"And so will this rhyme from Morgan," said Kathleen. She pulled a small piece of parchment paper from her cloak and gave it to Annie.

Annie read the words on the paper aloud.

> *To Jack and Annie of Frog Creek:*
>
> *Though the question is quite simple,*
> *Simple answers might be wrong.*
> *If you want to know the right one,*
> *Help the genius all day long,*
> *Morning, noon, and afternoon,*
> *Till the night bird sings its song.*

"So to find the secret of happiness, we need to spend the whole day helping Leonardo da Vinci," said Jack.

"Yes," said Kathleen. Teddy nodded.

"I wish you could come, too," said Annie.

"And help *us*," said Jack.

"Never fear," said Kathleen. "You will have the help of the great genius and the Wand of Dianthus."

"Oh!" Annie said to Jack. "Did you bring our wand?"

"Of course," said Jack. "I always carry it with me for safekeeping." He reached into his backpack and pulled out a gleaming silver wand.

"The Wand of Dianthus," Teddy said in a hushed voice.

The wand looked like the horn of a unicorn. It burned in Jack's hand—with cold or warmth, he couldn't tell which. He carefully put the wand back into his pack.

"Remember the three rules of the wand?" said Kathleen.

"Sure," said Annie. "You can only use it for the good of others. You can only use it after you've tried your hardest. And you can only use it with a command of *five* words."

"Excellent," said Kathleen.

"Thanks," said Annie. "Ready?" she asked Jack.

Jack nodded. "Bye, Teddy. Bye, Kathleen."

"Good-bye," said Teddy.

"And good luck," said Kathleen.

Jack pointed at the cover of the book. "I wish we could go to Leonardo da Vinci!"

In the distance, the school bell started to ring, letting kids know that school would start in ten minutes. But in the Frog Creek woods, the wind started to blow.

The tree house started to spin.

It spun faster and faster.

Then everything was still.

Absolutely still.

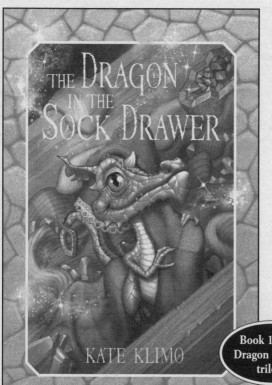

Discover the facts
behind the fiction with the

MAGIC TREE HOUSE®
RESEARCH GUIDES

The must-have, all-true companions for your
favorite Magic Tree House® adventures!

Guess what?

Jack and Annie are going on the stage!

For more information on
MAGIC TREE HOUSE: THE MUSICAL
(including how to order the CD!), visit
www.mthmusical.com.

Sal Murdocca is best known for his amazing work on the Magic Tree House series. He has written and/or illustrated over two hundred children's books, including *Dancing Granny* by Elizabeth Winthrop, *Double Trouble in Walla Walla* by Andrew Clements, and *Big Numbers* by Edward Packard. He has taught writing and illustration at the Parsons School of Design in New York. He is the librettist for a children's opera and has recently completed his second short film. Sal Murdocca is an avid runner, hiker, and bicyclist. He has often bicycle-toured in Europe and has had many one-man shows of his paintings from these trips. He lives and works with his wife, Nancy, in New City, New York.